WEEKLY READER CHILDREN'S BOOK CLUB PRESENTS

S. Campbell

THE
LITTLE
TINY ROOSTER

PICTURE BOOKS BY *Will and Nicolas*

THE TWO REDS

FINDERS KEEPERS
(Caldecott Award Winner, 1952)

EVEN STEVEN

THE CHRISTMAS BUNNY

CIRCUS RUCKUS

CHAGA

PERRY THE IMP

SLEEPYHEAD

THE MAGIC FEATHER DUSTER

FOUR-LEAF CLOVER

THE LITTLE TINY ROOSTER

Will and Nicolas

HARCOURT, BRACE & WORLD, INC., NEW YORK

Little tiny rooster crow
for Barbara

Hardbound edition ISBN 0-15-247577-X
Library edition ISBN 0-15-247578-8

Library of Congress Catalog Number: 60-12309
Printed in the United States of America

Weekly Reader Children's Book Club Edition
Primary Division

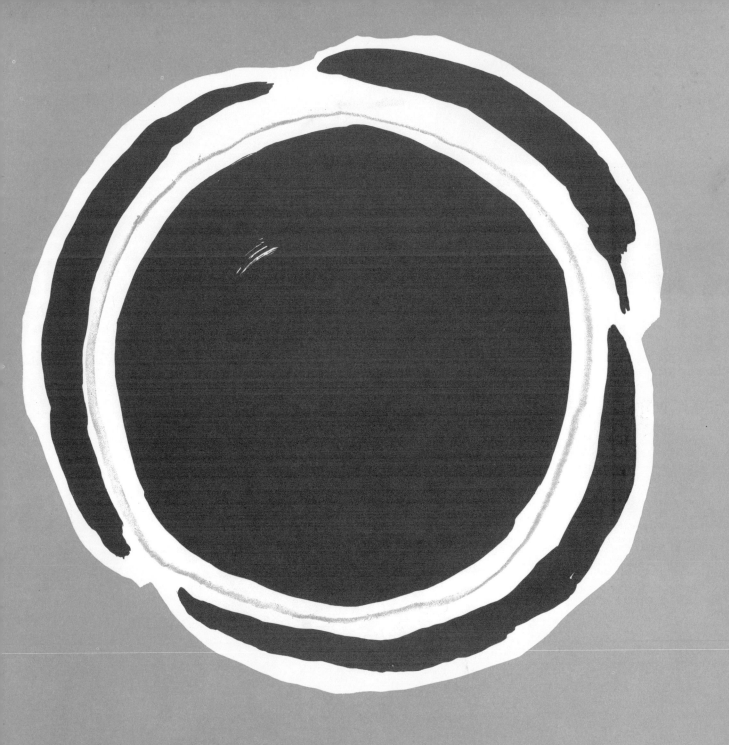

At the first peep of dawn the farmyard leader
stretched out his neck and crowed:
    "Break-of-day, break-of-day, wake!"
This was the signal for the farm day to begin.

And it began like any other day in the spring.
The chickens strutted around the yard, stopping
now and then to scratch for worms. The ducks
waddled down to the pond and swam off in a line.

The horses and cows nibbled at the grass in the near field. The dogs ran back and forth barking, then settled down to their morning nap. The cats were already asleep. They had been out all night.

In the henhouse the mother hen was hatching out eggs. Hidden among the others was an egg the size of a walnut. The chicks began to peck their way out of their shells. The mother hen hovered over them, helping. Suddenly the little tiny egg cracked. A little tiny chick stepped out. The mother hen picked off a bit of shell that still clung to it and said: "Call this a chick? Why, it's no bigger than a grasshopper!"

By summer the little tiny chick had grown into
a little tiny rooster, complete from comb to
spurs. He was as cocky as a rooster can be.
But he was different from the others. He made
friends with the dogs.

He flew up
into the air
and lighted on
a horse's back.
And the horse,
not minding at all,
took him for a ride
around the field.

The cats had been taught to leave the chickens alone, and they did. But they liked to talk to the little tiny rooster because he listened so well. They told him about their nights in the woods and the hunting in the dark.

The cows kept to themselves and minded their own business. But when the little tiny rooster passed and crowed a friendly greeting, they mooed softly in answer.

Only the chickens made things hard. At mealtimes they rushed to the trough, crowding and pushing. Nobody made room for the little tiny rooster.

body was settled in his place. The barnyard leader spoke.
"...er hen tells me that some of our eggs are missing.
...shall we do?" The hens and the ducks set up such a clucking
...uacking that they seemed about to burst.
...were angry enough. What they couldn't say was what to do.

At night they lined up to roost. The little tiny
rooster tried to find a place. The others shoved
him aside without even seeming to notice him.

One morning the barnyard leader flew to th[e]
the fence and crowed three times to call a c[...]
All the chickens came running. The ducks [...]
from the pond, shaking the water from the[ir]
The horses leaned over the fence. The cows [...]
behind, chewing their cuds. The dogs sat o[n...]
haunches and looked wise. The cats preten[ded...]
were asleep but listened all the same.

Ever[...]
"Mo[...]
Wha[...]
and [...]
They[...]

The old gray horse was the first to think of something.
"Why don't you have a watchman?" he said.
"Just what we need," said the barnyard leader. "Somebody
with sharp eyes who can stay up all night and watch
without snatching even a wink of sleep."

"I can do it," said the little tiny rooster.
"Let me be watchman."
"No, me!" "Let me!" "I can!" the other young
roosters shouted, all speaking at once.

The barnyard leader looked at them. "Little
tiny rooster, you're too small," he said.
He chose three of the others and gave each
a post up on the rafters of the henhouse.

The little tiny rooster walked off sadly.
"No chance here for me," he thought. "I'm too small."
And he started down the road away from the farm.
On and on he trudged, planning what he would do
in the great world. He came to a fork in the road
and stopped. "This way or that, does it matter
which I choose?" he thought. "Nothing I find in
the world will make up for what I left on the farm."
And he turned back, saying to himself: "After all,
the farm is my home. Let the others do as they like;
I will do my part."

Just as the sun was setting, the little tiny rooster
reached the henhouse. He did not stop to eat or drink.

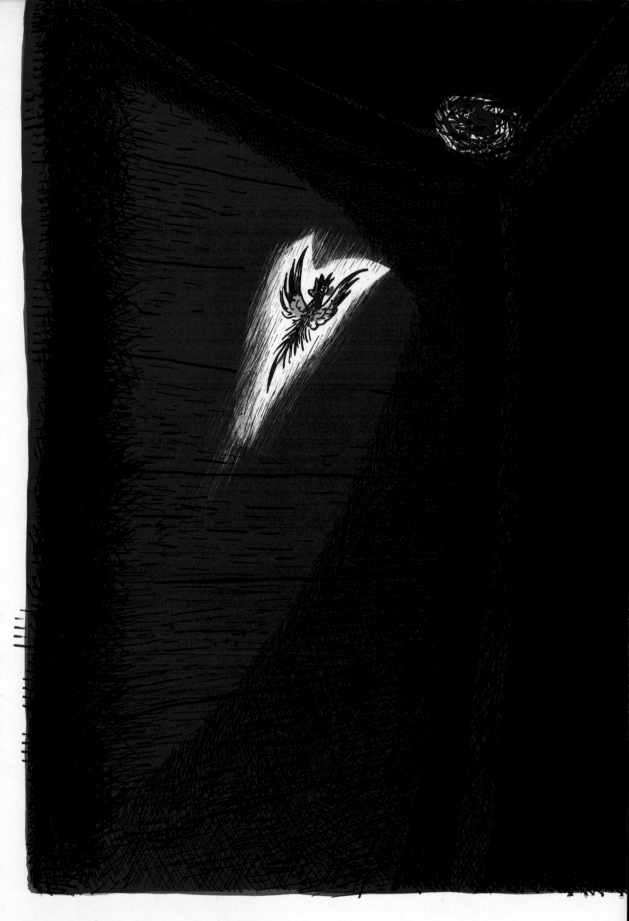

He went in and looked around. High at the top he saw an old swallows' nest. He flew straight up and hid in the nest.

In the middle of the night,
one by one,
the young roosters
who had been set to watch
dropped off to sleep.
The little tiny rooster
kept stoutly awake
and watched
from his hiding place above.
The fox, seeing
the watchmen asleep,
crept in
without making a sound.
The little tiny rooster
stretched out his neck . . .
and crowed the call of alarm:
"Chicken-and-chick,
come quick, come quick!"
The chickens woke with a start.

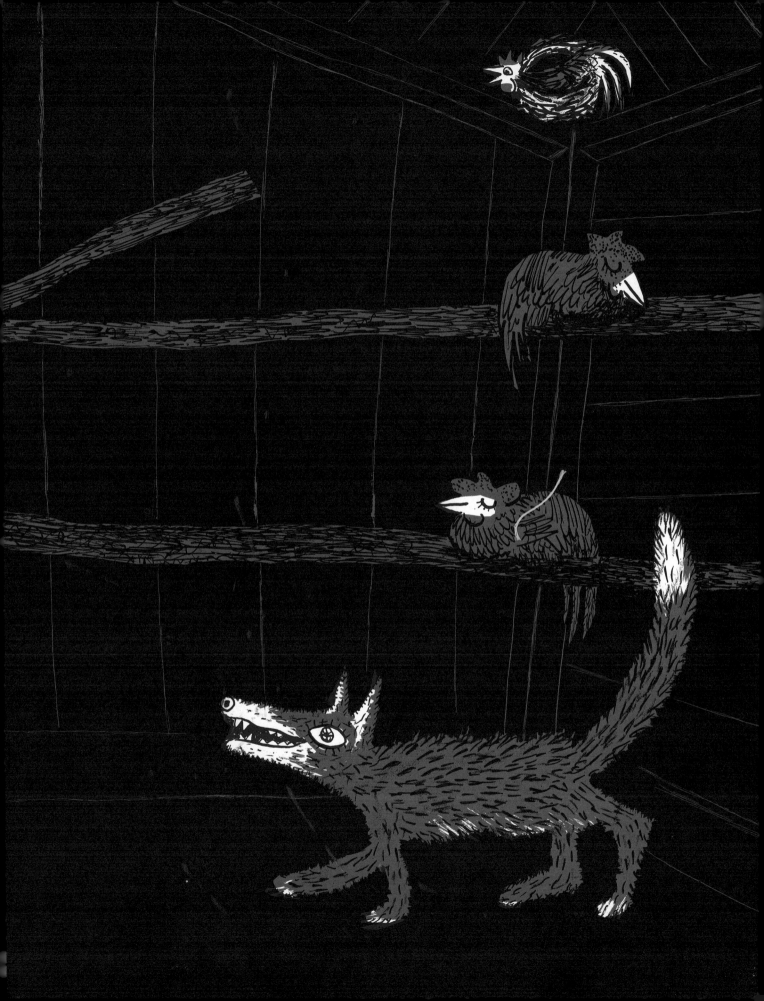

They went at the fox. Their beaks pecked
and poked at him from every side.
The din they made was deafening.

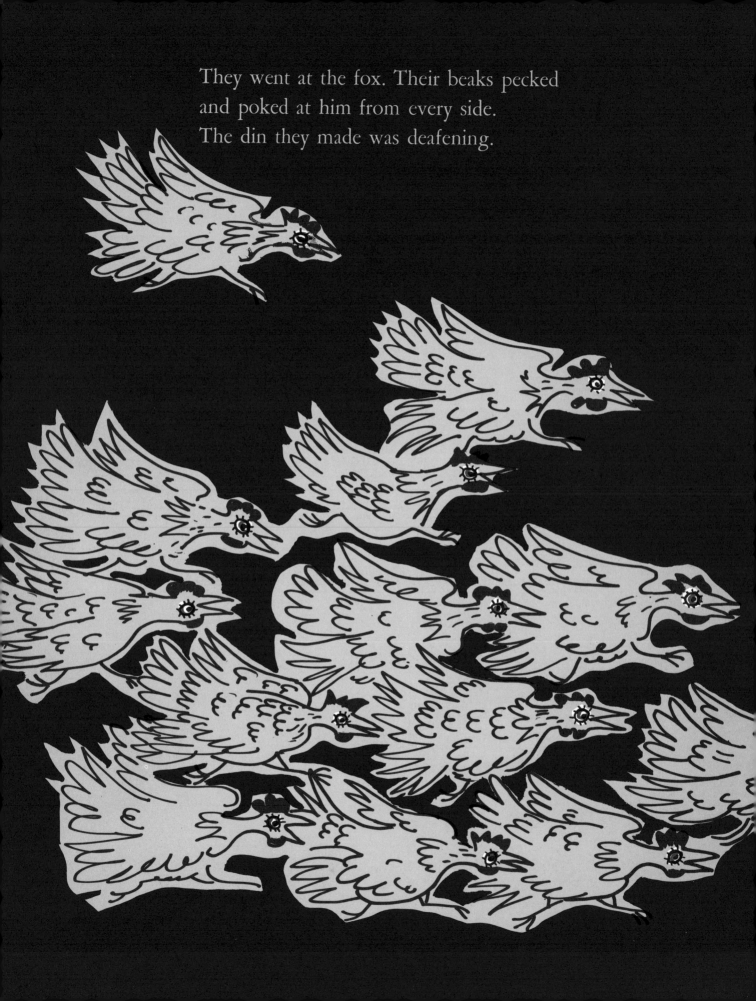

The fox ran out of the henhouse. Now the dogs were at him, barking and snapping. He ran into the field. Horses and cows came thundering down upon him, snorting and stamping their hoofs.

The fox dashed away as fast as he could go,
saying to himself: "Such a deal of noise
over nothing. If I get off safe, I'll never
come near this place again."

The next morning two roosters stood ready
to give the signal for the farm day to begin.
"You and I together, little tiny rooster,"
said the barnyard leader. And they stretched
out their necks and crowed together:
  "Break-of-day, break-of-day, wake!"